# Emeline at the Circus

## Marjorie Priceman

Alfred A. Knopf, New York

$\mathcal{E}$meline's teacher, Ms. Splinter, said the circus would be a great learning experience. Ms. Splinter should know, because Ms. Splinter knows everything.

As soon as the second grade was seated, Ms. Splinter gave them instructions on how to enjoy the circus.

"Sit up straight. No shouting. No fighting. No fidgeting. No standing on the seats. No wandering off. If you get lost, you'll spend the circus in the Lost and Found—a dark little room with no windows. You'll miss *everything*.

"Now SHHHHHHHHHH! The circus is starting."

"Ahhh! The intelligent elephant.

Resident of Africa and India. An African elephant has larger ears than an Indian elephant. Both are endangered. Both are enormous. The African elephant stands up to twelve feet tall. Weighs up to eight tons. With its long trunk, the elephant can reach food high above its head."

"I call your attention to the llama—scientific name, *Lama glama*. A member of the

camel family, native to South America. The llama can be seen climbing nimbly up mountain trails. Her favorite food is grass."

"Ha! The delightful clowns!

According to the dictionary,

clown comes from the Old

Norse word *klönne*, meaning

'clumsy fellow.' Now, sit still,

class, hands on laps. Let's leave

the clowning to the clowns."

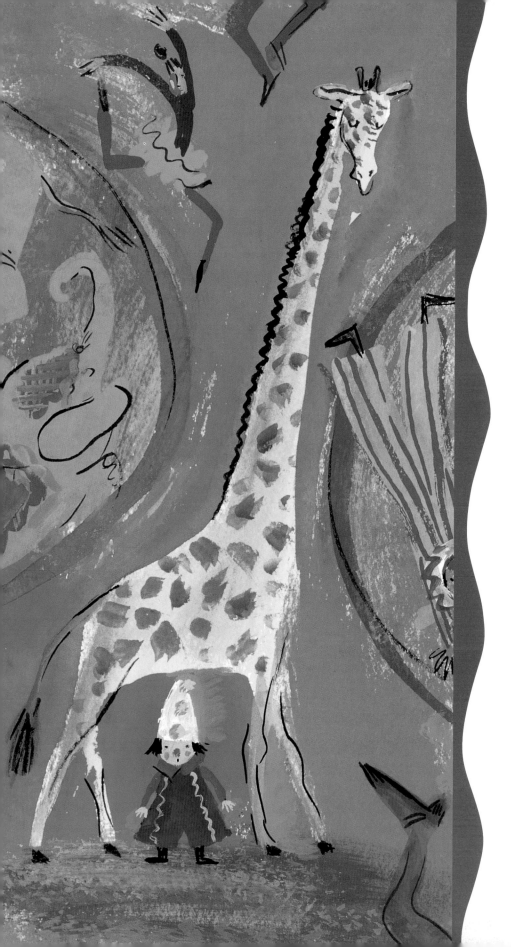

"Notice the stately giraffe.

Tallest animal on earth. A relative of the deer. The giraffe is a vegetarian, dining on the tops of acacia and mimosa trees."

"Observe the graceful horse.

Latin name, *Equus*. A hoofed,

herbivorous mammal. Relative

of the zebra and donkey.

Horses travel in herds."

"Hail the clever monkey.

Close relative to that other clever creature, the second grader. There are two hundred monkey varieties. Some have prehensile tails for swinging from trees. Many have highly developed hands and feet— although they rarely form brass bands in the wild."

"That, children, is fire—a phenomenon of combustion manifested in light, flame,

and heat. According to the dictionary, a fire-eater is someone who pretends to eat fire."

"My word! The mighty hippopotamus. River-dwelling fellow of tropical Africa.

Distant cousin to the pig. Hippos have eyes on top of their heads so they can see while lying in the water."

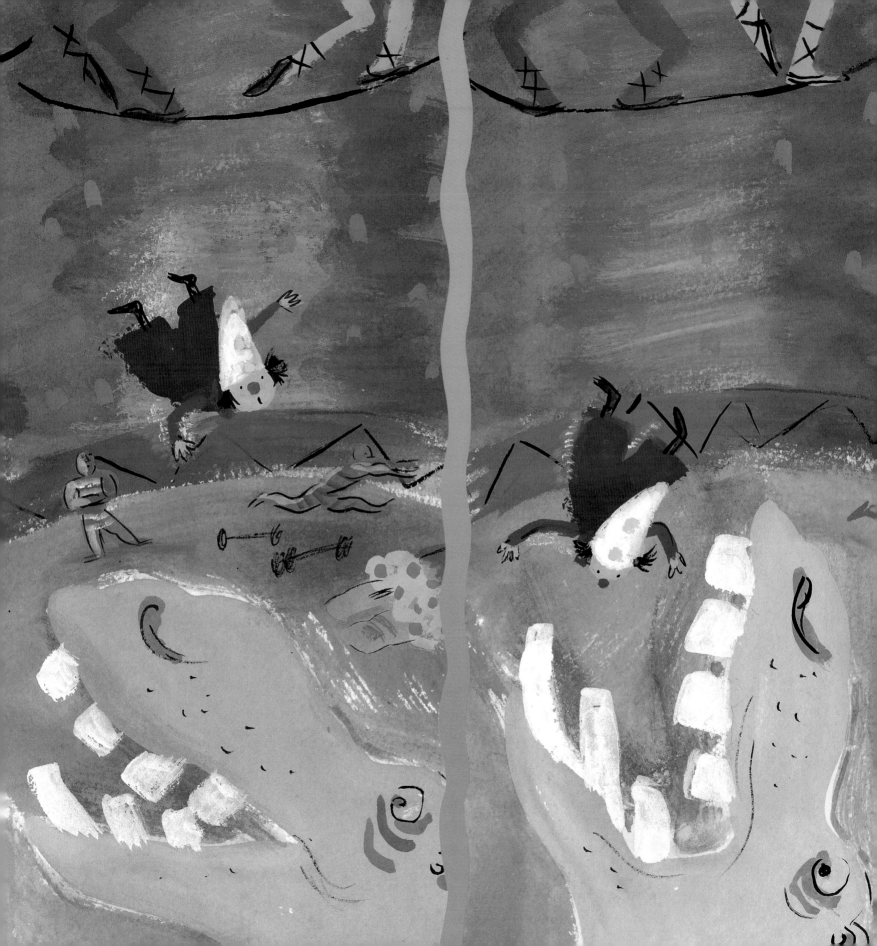

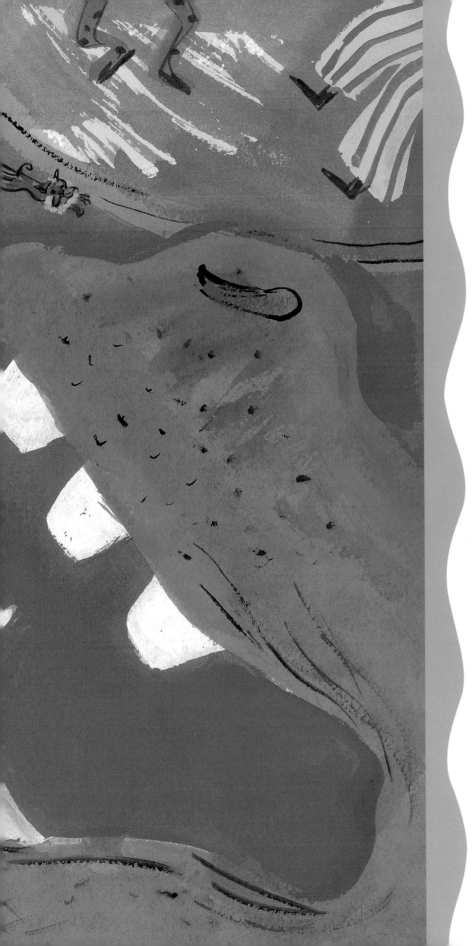

"Behold the powerful strongman! He is able to lift heavy objects using his

*deltoids*, which are the shoulder muscles, his *biceps*, which are the muscles on the front of the upper arm, and his *triceps*, the muscles on the back of the upper arm."

"Consider the tiger. Member of the cat family. Nocturnal hunter in the forests of Asia.

Endangered species. Tigers are carnivores with sharp front teeth for biting and chewing. They are good swimmers but poor climbers."

"Don't miss the sprightly acrobats! According to the dictionary, acrobat comes from

the Greek word *akróbatos*, which means 'walking on tiptoe.' These are highly skilled professionals with years of training. Do not attempt these stunts yourself."

"I direct your attention to the daring trapeze artist!

The trapeze is an acrobatic apparatus consisting of a short horizontal bar suspended by two parallel ropes. Pay attention . . ."

"What a splendid stunt!"                    "What an expert aerialist!"

"What a brave little . . ."

"EMELINE!?!"

The End

# For Elizabeth and Jonathan

THIS IS A BORZOI BOOK PUBLISHED BY ALFRED A. KNOPF, INC.

Copyright © 1999 by Marjorie Priceman

www.randomhouse.com/kids

*Library of Congress Cataloging-in-Publication Data*
Priceman, Marjorie
Emeline at the circus / by Marjorie Priceman. — 1st ed. p. cm.
Summary: While her teacher Miss Splinter is lecturing her second-grade class
about exotic animals, clowns, and other performers they are watching
at the circus, Emeline accidentally becomes part of the show.
[1. Circus - - Fiction.   2. School field trips - - Fiction.
3. Teachers - - Fiction]  I. Title.
PZ7. P932E1   1999

ISBN 0-679-87685-5 (trade)
0-679-97685-X (lib. bdg.)

Printed in Hong Kong

10  9  8  7  6  5  4  3  2  1

FIRST EDITION